Pablo Picks His Shoes

Pablo created by Gráinne Mc Guinness

Written by Rosie King

LADYBIRD BOOKS

UK | USA | Canada | Ireland | Australia | India | New Zealand | South Africa

Ladybird Books is part of the Penguin Random House group of companies
whose addresses can be found at global.penguinrandomhouse.com.

www.penguin.co.uk   www.puffin.co.uk   www.ladybird.co.uk

Penguin
Random House
UK

First published 2020
001

Text and illustrations copyright © Paper Owl Creative, 2020
Pablo copyright © Paper Owl Creative, 2015

PAPER OWL FILMS

Printed in China

A CIP catalogue record for this book is available from the British Library

ISBN: 978-0-241-41575-7

All correspondence to:
Ladybird Books
Penguin Random House Children's
One Embassy Gardens, New Union Square
5 Nine Elms Lane, London SW8 5DA

Tang

Noa

Draff

I'm Pablo!

Llama

Mouse

Wren

These are my friends, the Book Animals!
The Book Animals live in the Art World,
where I draw my stories.

One day, I was getting ready to **go out**. Mum was taking me to Granny's house, and Tang was helping me to pack.

"Can I come, too?" asked Wren.
"**Of course!**" I said. "We can all go!"

The Book Animals were all excited.
"You mean we don't have to take turns?"
asked Noasaurus.
"We don't have to take turns," repeated Llama.

"Yaaaay!" cheered the Book Animals. They were very happy that they could all go together.

We were almost ready to go, when I heard a small shout . . .

"Take us! Take us!" shouted a pair of blue shoes, hopping up and down.

"Why are those shoes making such a racket?" asked Draff.
"They want to come out with us, Draff," I said.
"Can we go on your feet now?" asked the pair of blue shoes.
But then we heard **another** shout . . .

"Take us! Take us!" shouted a pair of
yellow shoes, jumping out of the cupboard.
"Not again!" said Draff.
"We're ready to come out with you!"
said the yellow shoes.

Then there was **another** shout!
"Hey, Pablo!" said a pair of red sandals.
"We're ready to go to Granny's house!"

"Now I don't know which of you to wear," I said. "I don't want to hurt anyone's feelings!"

"But they're **shoes**!" said Draff. "They don't actually have any feelings, in point of fact."
"Well, excuse me!" said a blue shoe. "How would you feel if I said giraffes don't have feelings?"

"I wish I could bring all of you," I said, "but I only have two feet!"
"Maybe **someone else** could wear us," said the yellow shoes, looking at the Book Animals.

Wren tried on the yellow shoes, but her feet were too small. When she tried to walk, she just fell over.

Noa tried to put on the red sandals,
but they ran away!
"We are not going out on **your** feet,
thank you very much!" they said.
"They are **way** too big!"

"Pablo's shoes only fit Pablo," said Mouse.
Then all of the shoes started shouting.

Tang had an idea. "Maybe Pablo can use his hands as an extra pair of feet!" he said. "I'm an orangutan, and sometimes we use our feet as hands!"

I put the red sandals on my **head** . . .

and the yellow shoes on my **hands** . . .

and the blue shoes on my **feet.**

Then we heard a shout from someone else!

Two more pairs of shoes appeared.
"Pick us! Pick us!"
called my big purple wellies.
"No, pick us, Pablo!"
called my brown shoes.

"This is just getting silly," said Draff.
"What do we do now?" asked Mouse.

"Pablo can draw himself two more pairs of legs," said
Wren. "Then he'll be able to wear all five pairs of shoes!"
But I couldn't draw anything with shoes on my hands!

I'd had enough. I shook off
all the shoes and ran away.

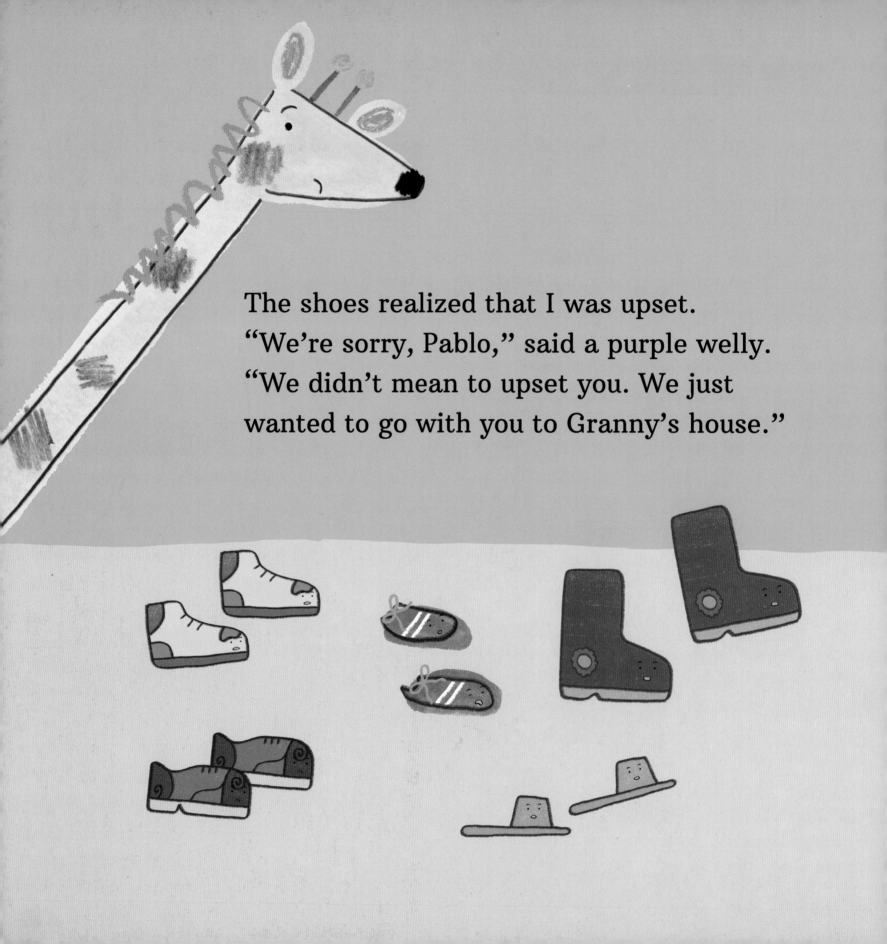

The shoes realized that I was upset.
"We're sorry, Pablo," said a purple welly.
"We didn't mean to upset you. We just
wanted to go with you to Granny's house."

"I'd take all of you with me if I could," I told them. "But I can't! And I don't like to **choose**!"

"We don't have to take turns," said Llama. "Good idea, Llama," said Mouse. "The shoes can take turns to go with Pablo!"

"Two of you can go today," said Noa, "and two others could go next time, and so on!"
Perfect! That's perfect!" called the shoes.
"But I still have to choose a pair of shoes to wear today!" I said.

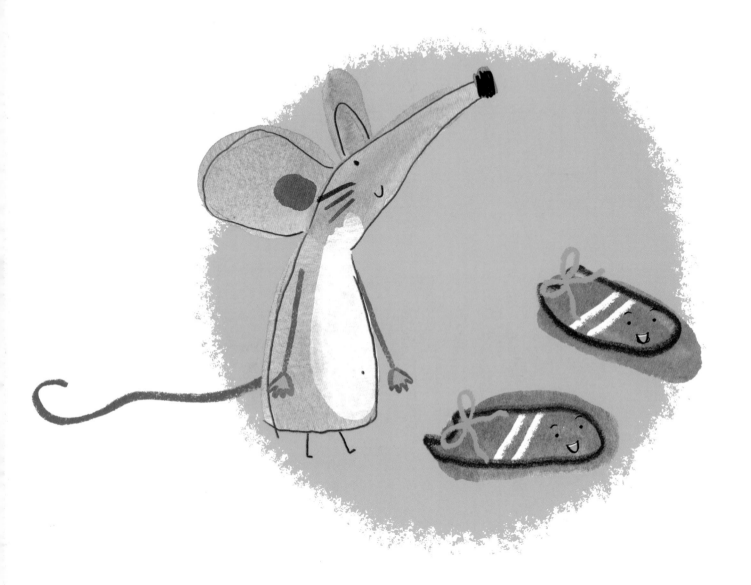

"Mouse thinks that the blue shoes were the first to ask," said Mouse. "Pablo should pick them first."
"Yaaay!" cheered the blue shoes.

So I went to my granny's house, with the blue shoes on my feet. We had a lovely time.

The other shoes were a little sad to be left on their own. But, with everyone else gone, they realized they could have a . . .

. . . shoe party!
So they all had fun
staying at home!

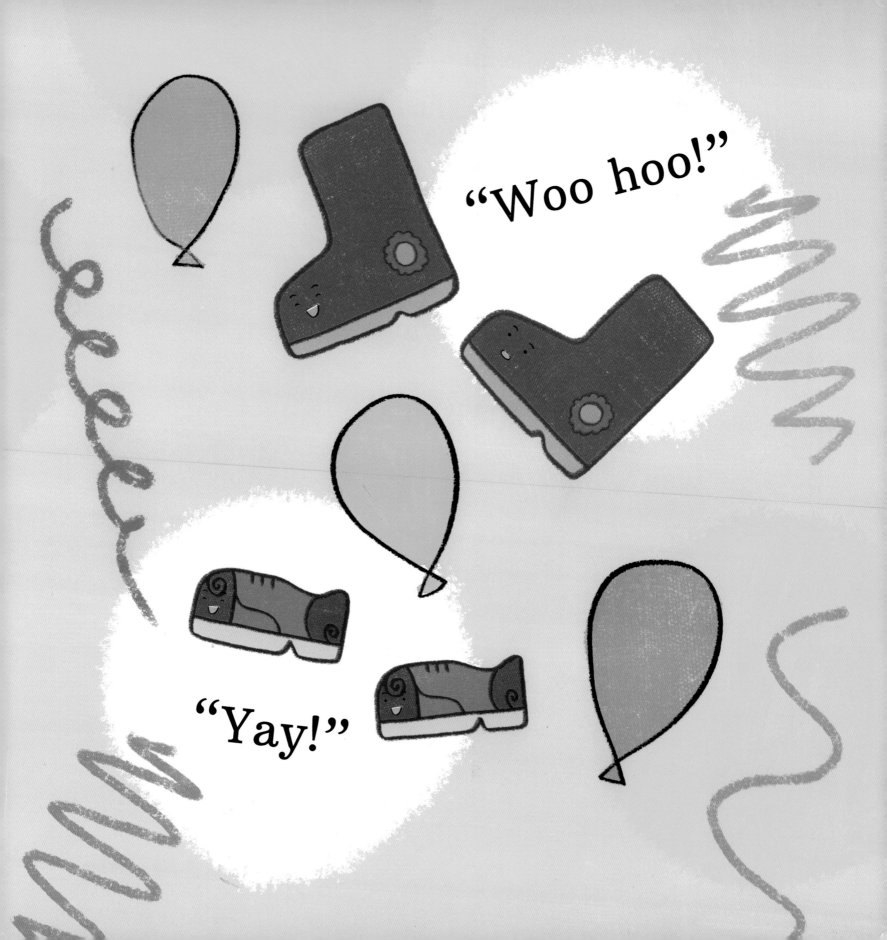

My blue shoes and I had a great time, too!